The Hungry Little Boy

by Joan W. Blos   illustrated by Dena Schutzer

SIMON & SCHUSTER BOOKS FOR YOUNG READERS

SIMON & SCHUSTER BOOKS FOR YOUNG READERS An imprint of Simon & Schuster Children's
Publishing Division, 1230 Avenue of the Americas, New York, New York 10020. Text copyright
© 1995 by Joan W. Blos. Illustrations copyright © 1995 by Dena Schutzer. All rights reserved
including the right of reproduction in whole or in part in any form. SIMON & SCHUSTER BOOKS FOR
YOUNG READERS is a trademark of Simon & Schuster. Book design by David Neuhaus. The text for
this book is set in 20-point Stone Sans Bold. The illustrations were done in oils. Manufactured
in the United States of America

10   9   8   7   6   5   4   3   2   1

Library of Congress Cataloging-in-Publication Data Blos, Joan W. The hungry little boy / Joan
W. Blos : illustrated by Dena Schutzer.   p. cm. Summary: A young boy enjoys the lunch that
his grandmother has carefully prepared. [1. Food habits—Fiction. 2. Grandmothers—Fiction.]
I. Schutzer, Dena, ill. II. Title. PZ7.B6237Hu 1995 [E]—dc20 94-6836 CIP AC
ISBN: 0-671-88128-0

For May
—J. W. B.

For David and Lisa
—D. S.

Once there was a hungry little boy.
So his grandma said to him,
"I will make you something to eat."

**She found bread
in the bread box**

**and milk
in the refrigerator**

**and peanut butter
in the cupboard**

**and carrots
in the vegetable bin**

and an apple

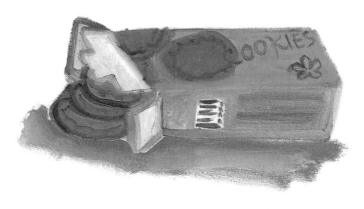

and some cookies.

And she found two plates and a cup.
And these she put on the table,
all ready and waiting.

Next she peeled the carrot
until it was smooth and shiny.
Then she cut it neatly
into pieces nice to eat.

She spread peanut butter
all over one of the slices of bread.
And she put the other slice of bread
on top of the first one
and she pressed them together.

She put the four carrot pieces
and the two sandwich halves
on the first plate.

And she put three cookies
and the one apple
on the other plate.

So then everything was ready,
and the little boy started to eat.
He ate the pieces of carrot.
Four.

And he drank some milk.

He ate the halves of the sandwich.
Two.

And he drank some milk.

He ate the cookies.
Three.

And he drank some milk.

But the one apple
he put into his pocket
because now he wasn't hungry,
but he might want it later.

Then the boy and his grandma went outside together.